ANIMAL PANTS!

For the children and staff at
Vale Infant School, Guernsey - B.M.

For my parents - A.B.

First published 2009 by Macmillan Children's Books
This edition published 2010 by Macmillan Children's Books
a division of Macmillan Publishers Limited
20 New Wharf Road, London N1 9RR
Basingstoke and Oxford
Associated companies throughout the world
www.panmacmillan.com

ISBN: 978-0-230-73614-6

Text copyright © Brian Moses 2009
Illustrations copyright © Anja Boretzki 2009
Moral Rights Asserted

3 5 7 9 8 6 4

A CIP catalogue record for this book is available from the British Library.

Printed in China

Brian Moses

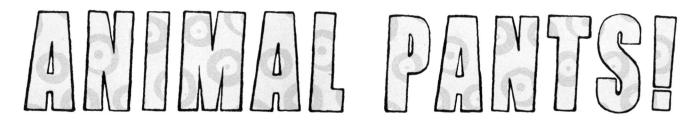

ANIMAL PANTS!

Illustrated by Anja Boretzki

MACMILLAN CHILDREN'S BOOKS

From the biggest gorillas to the tiniest ants,

the animals are wearing
UNDERPANTS!

A warthog's pants
barely cover his belly,

a skunk's underpants
are really smelly.

a chameleon's change
from red to green.

A kangaroo's pants
are full of fleas,

a frog wears his pants
when he's off for a jog.

A hippo's pants will make you grin,